D0207092

Praise for The Imagination Station books

Our children have been riveted and on the edge of their seats through each and every chapter of The Imagination Station books. The series is well-written, engaging, family friendly, and has great spiritual truths woven into the stories. Highly recommended!

—Crystal P., *Money Saving Mom*®

[The Imagination Station books] focus on God much more than the Magic Tree House books do.

—Emilee, age 7, Waynesboro, Pennsylvania

These books will help my kids enjoy history.

—Beth S., third-grade public school teacher
Colorado Springs, Colorado

These books are a great combination of history and adventure in a clean manner perfect for young children.

—Margie B., *My Springfield Mommy* blog

To Amy Green,

who fought Nazis from her

cubicle every day this summer.

—MKH

FOCUS ON THE FAMILY® PRESENTS

THE IMAGINATION STATION®

Escape to the Hiding Place

BOOK 9

MARIANNE HERING • MARSHAL YOUNGER
CREATIVE DIRECTION BY PAUL McCUSKER
ILLUSTRATED BY DAVID HOHN

TYNDALE

FOCUS ON THE FAMILY • ADVENTURES IN ODYSSEY
TYNDALE HOUSE PUBLISHERS, INC. • CAROL STREAM, ILLINOIS

Escape to the Hiding Place
Copyright © 2012 by Focus on the Family. All rights reserved.

ISBN: 978-1-58997-693-1

A Focus on the Family book published by Tyndale House Publishers, Inc., Carol Stream, Illinois 60188

Focus on the Family and Adventures in Odyssey, and the accompanying logos and designs, are federally registered trademarks, and The Imagination Station is a federally registered trademark of Focus on the Family, Colorado Springs, CO 80995.

TYNDALE and Tyndale's quill logo are registered trademarks of Tyndale House Publishers, Inc.

All Scripture quotations marked are taken from New King James Version®, (NKJV™). Copyright © 1982 by Thomas Nelson, Inc. Used by permission. All rights reserved.

No part of this publication may be reproduced, stored in a retrieval system, or transmitted in any form or by any means—electronic, mechanical, photocopy, recording, or otherwise—without prior written permission of Focus on the Family.

With the exception of known historical figures, all characters are the product of the authors' imaginations.

Cover design by Michael Heath | Magnus Creative

Cataloging-in-Publication Data for this book is available by contacting the Library of Congress at http://www.loc.gov/help/contact-general.html.

Printed in the United States of America
2 3 4 5 6 7 8 9 / 16 15 14 13

For manufacturing information regarding this product, please call 1-800-323-9400.

Contents

The Ice-Cream Shop

Cousins Beth and Patrick sat at the counter of Whit's End ice-cream shop.

"Hello, Patrick and Beth. How may I help you?" Whit asked. He smiled at them.

Beth sighed. "I'll have a scoop of chocolate ice cream, please," she said.

Patrick said, "I'm not really hungry. A root beer, I guess."

"Patrick? Not hungry?" Whit said. "Well, that's something new. Is everything all right?"

Patrick looked at Beth. He said, "Go on, *you* tell him."

Beth took a deep breath. Then she said, "Patrick and I wanted to babysit and help in the church nursery. So our parents told us to take a class with the Red Cross first."

"We even found first-aid stuff on the Red Cross website," Patrick said. "We know what to do during an earthquake."

"And that we should chop up hot dogs before giving them to toddlers," Beth said.

Whit said, "And so . . ."

"We went to sign up for the Red Cross class," Patrick said. "But you have to be eleven to take it."

"And no one will let us help without the class," Beth said. "What a waste of time."

Whit set a root beer in front of Patrick.

The foam dripped down the side of the tall glass.

"So do you think that reading about first aid was a waste?" Whit asked.

Patrick shrugged. He took a long sip of the drink.

"I guess not," Beth said. "I mean, I learned a lot. But now I feel useless. It'll be forever until I'm eleven!"

"Forever?" Whit asked. "In this case, forever is three years. And you're right. By then, you'll be an ancient fifth grader."

Whit scooped Beth's chocolate ice cream into a pretty glass dish. He placed it on the counter in front of her.

Beth took a spoon and dug into the chocolate mound. "No one thinks kids can do anything," she said.

Patrick said, "Except empty the trash and clean the cat litter box."

Whit chuckled. "Oh, I don't believe that's the case," he said. "I know many children who did great things. Just look in your history book or your Bible. Some kids have been kings, queens, or emperors."

"But I'm not King Patrick," Patrick said.

"What can I do?"

"And I'm not even allowed to cross Oak Street without an adult," Beth said.

Whit's eyes sparkled. Patrick could tell Whit had an idea.

"After you finish your ice cream and soda," Whit said, "meet me in the workshop. I think this is the perfect time for a trip in the Imagination Station."

● ● ●

Beth and Patrick had been in the Imagination Station before. It was like a time machine. They never knew when or where in history they were going. But they always knew they were in for an adventure.

Beth and Patrick stepped inside. Each sat in one of the two chairs. Lights, numbers, and buttons stretched out across the panel in front of them. Patrick thought it looked like a helicopter cockpit.

"Are you ready?" Whit's voice came in on a small speaker.

"Yes, sir," the cousins said.

"Then push the red button and hang on," Whit said.

Beth pressed the button. The machine shook.

Patrick felt like the Imagination Station would pull loose from the ground.

There was a loud rumble.

Then everything went dark.

The Plane Crash

Patrick's eyes adjusted to the darkness of the Imagination Station. Then everything was flooded with light. He squinted and looked around.

He and Beth were sitting cross-legged on the shore of a beautiful lake. They were surrounded by trees. Across the lake, a narrow piece of land jutted into the water. A small windmill sat on the land. Its blades turned slowly in the wind.

"Wow! Nice place," Beth said. She looked at her clothes. They were different now. She wore an olive-green dress.

Patrick looked down and noticed his clothing. He wore a white shirt and an olive-green jacket. His pants matched the jacket.

Something was on his head. He reached up and pulled off a green cap.

Patrick put the cap back on. Then he noticed a thin red scarf. It made his neck itch. Annoyed, he moved the scarf's knot to one side.

"Hey, look at my watch!" Beth said. "It's not my pink one with the plastic band." She held out her wrist to show a black velvet watchband. The watch face had diamonds around the edges.

"Are those real diamonds?" Patrick asked.

"Maybe," Beth said. "But the watch is broken. The hands aren't moving."

"Why would Mr. Whittaker program the Imagination Station to give you a broken watch?" Patrick asked.

Beth shrugged. Then she said, "Where do you think we are?"

"Well, we're not wearing Roman tunics," Patrick said. "Or Pilgrim outfits. These clothes almost look normal."

Patrick thought for a moment. "When were windmills invented?" he asked.

"I don't know," Beth said. "The Middle Ages? But they didn't have watches then, did they?"

Patrick leaned back and felt something press against his back. He turned around. A backpack sat on the ground just behind him.

"What's this?" he asked.

Before Beth could answer, a sound caught their attention. At first Patrick thought it was a lawnmower in the distance.

Beth pointed at the sky. "It's a plane," she said.

Patrick glanced over. She was right. A small airplane appeared above the trees. It had blue, white, and red circles painted on the side.

The engine sputtered. The wings dipped.

Patrick stood up. Smoke trailed from the back of the plane.

"What's happening?" Beth asked.

"It's gonna crash!" Patrick shouted.

The plane zoomed overhead. Something

shot up out of the plane's cockpit.
And then the plane disappeared
beyond the trees across the lake.

A loud *CRASH* sounded, and the ground
shook. Smoke filled the sky above the trees.

"Look!" Beth said, pointing. A man with a
parachute hovered above the trees.

"It's the pilot!" Patrick said. "Let's go see if
he needs help!"

Beth was already running toward the
pilot.

Patrick raced after her along the water's
edge.

Patrick looked for the pilot as he ran. But
he couldn't see the parachute. Now
the trees blocked his view.

Suddenly, Beth
stopped.

Patrick almost plowed
into her. "What's wrong?"
Patrick asked.

"Listen," she said.

Patrick stood   still and
listened. He heard   a dog
barking.

"Look!" Beth said. She pointed toward the woods.

Three soldiers in gray uniforms moved through the trees. They had German shepherds with them. The large dogs were on leather leashes. The men had rifles slung across their backs.

The pack of men and dogs moved quickly. They were coming toward Patrick and Beth.

"This doesn't look good," Patrick said.

"Maybe we should hide," Beth said. The cousins scanned the area.

Patrick pointed to a clump of thick bushes. "There," he said.

The cousins ducked behind the bushes. Patrick was glad they both were wearing green. It was easier to blend in.

Beth peered between some leaves. "I can't

see them," she whispered.

"If you don't quiet down," a low muffled voice behind them said, "they'll find us for sure."

Beth gasped. She started to turn around.

"Whatever you do, don't move," the voice said.

Patrick froze. *Is it the pilot?* he wondered. "Who are you?" Patrick whispered.

"No time for questions now," the voice said. "Keep an eye on those soldiers."

Patrick obeyed. *I hope the dogs can't smell us,* he thought.

One of the soldiers shouted, but Patrick couldn't hear all the words. Then the soldier pointed across the lake.

That's where the plane went down, Patrick thought.

One of the dogs stopped. It sniffed the air and whined. Then it started moving . . . right toward Patrick and Beth!

Bernard

Beth wanted to run. But she knew it was too late. The dog had spotted them.

The voice said softly, "Stay still, no matter what."

Beth heard a sudden *kabang* in the distance. It sounded like an explosion. Except Beth thought she heard breaking glass, too.

The dog jerked toward the noise. It barked and pulled on its leash . . . away from the cousins and the stranger.

Beth peered back through the opening in the bushes. The soldiers ran toward the *kabang*.

What made that sound? Beth wondered. *Is it from the plane?*

Soon the sounds of footsteps and barks faded.

"It's safe," the voice said.

The bushes rustled as the three of them crawled out. They stood up carefully.

Beth looked to see who had been talking to them. She put a hand to her mouth in surprise.

She looked at a fair-skinned young woman. She was wearing a flowered dress. Her head was covered with a matching blue head scarf. Beth could see a hint of blush and lipstick on her face.

"Is it Halloween?" Patrick asked. "Why are you in a dress?"

Of course! Beth thought. *It's not a woman, but a young man dressed as a woman.*

The young man pulled the scarf away from his face. "My name is Bernard," he said.

"Why are you in a dress?" Patrick asked again.

"It's a disguise," Bernard said. "A woman is less likely to be captured and sent away to the work camps."

"Work camps?" Beth asked. "What's going on here?"

"I'll explain as we walk toward

Warmond," Bernard said. "You don't want to be caught or they'll send you away, too." He strode off.

Beth looked at Patrick. He shrugged. They followed the stranger.

"I wanted to find the pilot and help him hide," Bernard said.

"By yourself?" Patrick asked.

"No, there are a lot of us. I'm a member of the Dutch Resistance," Bernard said. He tied the scarf on his head again. "We're fighting the Nazis who invaded Holland."

Beth was alarmed. "The Nazis! Is that who we are hiding from?"

Bernard nodded. "The German soldiers are everywhere now."

Patrick frowned. "Is this World War Two?"

Bernard looked puzzled. "Is that what they're calling it?" he asked.

"Now I understand about the work camps," Beth said. She remembered from history how people died there.

"Let's talk about that later. Right now we have to get away from here," Bernard said. "There are too many soldiers in the woods around Warmond."

"What about the pilot?" Patrick asked.

"My father and other Resistance workers are looking for him too," Bernard said. "They'll find him. But right now we need to leave. It's too dangerous."

"Then where are we going?" Patrick asked.

Bernard said, "Let's walk around the lake toward the windmill. That leads to a road. But act normal. Walk slowly so it looks like we're out for a stroll. Otherwise . . ."

"Otherwise *what*?" Beth asked.

"The Germans might think we're up to something and shoot us," Bernard said.

The three slowly made their way around the lake.

Beth tried not to giggle at Bernard's strange clothes. He looked silly.

Bernard led them around to the windmill. Beth watched the large blades turn. They made a slight breeze. The windmill made a clacking sound every time it turned.

"Halt!" a voice called out suddenly.

The cousins and Bernard whirled around. They saw a lone German soldier coming toward them.

Bernard lowered his face and moved behind Patrick and Beth.

The German soldier pointed his long rifle right at Patrick. On the tip of the barrel was a sharp silver blade. It came within inches of Patrick's nose.

"What are you doing here?" the soldier shouted.

New Identities

Patrick's eyes focused on the sharp blade. He had to think quickly.

Patrick glanced at Bernard. Bernard kept his face turned away.

"We're just out for a walk," Patrick said finally.

"Did you see the plane?" the soldier asked. He spoke in a German accent. The word *see* sounded more like *zee*.

"Yes," Patrick said. "We saw a plane. It

crashed over there." He pointed to the other side of the lake.

"And the pilot?" the soldier asked.

Patrick shook his head. "We don't know where he landed."

Bernard still stared at the ground. Patrick knew he didn't want to speak. His deep voice would reveal that he wasn't a woman.

Beth's breathing was fast and shallow. She looked wide-eyed and frightened.

"Where are your papers?" the soldier asked.

Patrick gulped. *What is he talking about?* he wondered.

Bernard pulled a pouch from around his neck. He opened it and took out a folded white piece of paper.

The soldier inspected it. "You are Berdina Vos?" he asked.

Bernard nodded. The soldier returned the card to Bernard. He gave Bernard a suspicious look. Then he turned to Patrick and said, "What about your papers?"

Patrick swallowed hard. Then he felt a slight tickle under his collar. He reached up and pulled a string out from under his shirt. A piece of cardboard with writing on it was tied to the string.

Is this what the soldier wants? he wondered.

Patrick slipped the string over his head. Then he handed the card to the soldier.

Before the soldier could ask, Beth had taken out her card on a string. She looked relieved.

Thank you, Mr. Whittaker, Patrick thought. *You thought of everything!*

The soldier examined both cards and said, "Patrick . . . and Elisabeth."

The soldier studied Beth. His eye stopped at her wrist. He grabbed it and looked over the watch. He looked as if he were going to steal it.

Then the soldier frowned. "Your watch is broken," he said and dropped her wrist. "The diamonds are fake."

Beth just nodded, still looking terrified.

"You must leave this area," the soldier said. "There is a Canadian airman in these woods. Our men were told to shoot on sight. They might mistake you for the enemy."

"Yes, sir," Patrick said. He breathed a sigh of relief.

The soldier marched away.

"That was close," Patrick said to Bernard.

"Very close," Bernard said. "The soldier is right. We need to leave."

"Where will we go?" Patrick asked.

"My family's farm," Bernard said. "We'll be safer there."

● ● ●

The trip to the farm was about two miles, but it felt like twenty to Patrick. He worried that a German soldier might jump out at any moment and stick a rifle in his face.

Bernard led the way. He took them back through the area where the Imagination Station had brought them. Patrick looked around for the backpack, but it wasn't there.

Next, Bernard hiked up a hill. Beth and Patrick hung back.

"I wonder what happened to that backpack," Patrick said.

"Maybe the Germans found it," Beth said.

Patrick sighed. "Mr. Whittaker sent it with us. He must have put something important inside," he said. "I'm sorry I lost it."

"Don't worry about it," Beth said. "There's nothing we can do about it now."

Bernard reached the top of the hill. Then suddenly, he broke into a run.

"I see something," Bernard shouted without turning around.

Bernard stopped at the bottom of the hill.

Patrick and Beth caught up to him, breathing hard. A mess of cords and white material was tangled in the rocks.

It was a parachute.

The Farmhouse

"I thought the pilot landed on the other side of the lake," Beth said.

"Me too," Bernard said. "Maybe he carried the parachute with him for a while. If he was hurt or wounded, it may have become too heavy."

Beth noticed a deep red stain on the parachute's fabric. "Look," she said, and held it up.

Patrick and Bernard studied the fabric.

"It's blood," Bernard said.

A knot of worry formed in Beth's stomach.

The three sat for a moment and considered the stain.

Bernard gestured down the road. "The pilot is ahead of us," he said. "That means he's at least well enough to move."

Bernard spread out the parachute. "Come on," he said. "Help me."

"What are you doing?" Beth asked.

"Fabric is hard to get," Bernard said. "The Germans have taken over all the factories. This could be useful."

Patrick and Beth knelt down. They began to fold the parachute. Beth rubbed a piece of the material on her skin. It felt like silk.

Bernard tucked the folded parachute under his arm. "Let's get to the farm, quick. I don't want to be caught with this."

● ● ●

The farmhouse was a simple rectangular building. Its white paint was chipped. The roof sagged.

A thin cow stood chewing in the front yard. Some white feathers littered the ground. Beth didn't notice any other signs of farm animals.

But there were lots of children outside. Several of them stopped playing and stared at Beth and Patrick as they approached.

The cousins followed Bernard through a door in the middle of the farmhouse.

They entered a kitchen.

Black pots and pans hung from a ceiling rack. A tall woman stood at the sink washing dishes. She didn't seem to notice them.

Bernard put the parachute on a table. Then he walked to the woman at the sink. He placed his arm around her shoulders.

She spun around. "Bernard!" she cried. "I didn't hear you come in. You frightened me."

"Mother, these are my new friends, Beth and Patrick. They helped me escape from a German soldier," Bernard said. "Elisabeth, Patrick . . . this is my mother, Mrs. Vos."

Mrs. Vos seemed friendly. Her wrinkled skin looked like a golden raisin. Her gray hair lay flat on her head.

"A soldier?" Mrs. Vos said. She looked worried.

"It's all right, Mother," Bernard said. "He only questioned us. We left right after that."

"Thank God you did," Mrs. Vos said. She turned to the cousins. "Where are you from? Do I know your parents?" she asked.

Patrick and Beth exchanged glances. Beth had no idea how to answer.

Patrick said, "No, you probably don't. And they're not here."

Beth said, "We're separated from them."

Mrs. Vos looked concerned. "Oh, yes, this war has done that to so many. Do you know where they are?"

"Far away," Beth said.

"I'm sorry," the woman said. "These are desperate times. Do you need a place to stay?"

"We do, ma'am," Patrick said.

"You're welcome to stay here for a while," she said.

"Thank you very much," Beth said.

Mrs. Vos led Beth and Patrick down one of the halls to a large room where they were to sleep.

There were about a dozen bunk beds. Beth noticed a little girl lying still on one of the beds. The girl's eyes seemed empty.

Bernard caught Beth's gaze. He leaned over to her. "That's Mara," he said softly. "She's Jewish. Her parents were taken a month ago."

"Taken where?" Beth asked.

Bernard said, "We think to the prison in Amersfoort. But . . . we hope they will escape before going to a concentration camp."

Beth's heart sank at the words *concentration camp*. She remembered these words from her history class at school. The Germans killed millions of Jews in the camps. Mara's parents were facing death, if they weren't already dead.

Beth didn't know what to say. She knelt down and said, "Hello, Mara."

Mara didn't reply.

Beth gently stroked Mara's long black hair.

At dinner, Beth and Patrick met more of Bernard's family and the guests. All in all, more than fifteen people sat at the long table. Half of them were children Beth's age, or younger.

Mr. Vos's seat was empty.

"My father is still looking for the pilot," Bernard said. He had changed out of the dress and into farm clothes.

"Let's pray they find him," Mrs. Vos said.

They lowered their heads while Mrs. Vos prayed for her husband, the missing pilot, and the food before them.

Afterward, the children quickly attacked the cabbage rolls on their plates. Beth watched them. *They're so hungry.*

She picked at her food. She peeked across the table at Patrick. He hadn't eaten much either.

Beth moved her cabbage roll to Mara's plate. Mara gave her a shy smile.

Just then, the front door swung open with a bang. Two men came in. The first had a full beard. He was propping up the other man with his shoulder.

Bernard said, "Dad!"

Mrs. Vos jumped up from her chair. "Frans? What happened?" she asked.

"I found the pilot," Mr. Vos said. "He was hiding in our barn."

Mr. Vos gently lowered the pilot to the floor. The pilot groaned. Blood soaked the pants of his uniform.

Mrs. Vos rushed over to tend to him.

"He's got a gash in his leg," Mr. Vos said. "The wound is already infected. If we don't get a doctor soon, he might—"

Mr. Vos stopped suddenly and glanced at the children. Beth knew what he was going to say. The pilot might die.

"I'll change into my disguise and get a message to Dr. Nowak," Bernard said, standing.

"But what if a soldier stops you?" Mrs. Vos asked. "Your voice will give you away. You need someone to speak for you."

She looked around the room at the faces, then paused on Patrick's. "Take Patrick with you."

"Me?" Patrick asked.

"Yes," Mrs. Vos said.

The pilot moaned again, and Mrs. Vos bit her lip. "And please hurry. There isn't much time."

The Pilot

It was dark outside. Patrick and Bernard had been gone a long time.

Beth sat with Mrs. Vos next to the wounded pilot. He slept on one of the beds in a corner of the big room.

"What will you do with the pilot when he gets well?" Beth asked. She tried to be quiet so she wouldn't wake him.

"We'll help him escape," Mrs. Vos said. "We've done it before."

Mrs. Vos pointed to a gray uniform lying on a chair. "We have a friend who's a policeman. He gave us a German uniform. It's a perfect disguise for the pilot."

That's when Beth noticed a brown leather backpack under the chair. It was the one Patrick had left in the woods.

"That backpack," Beth said. "How did it get here?"

"I found it," a weak voice said.

It was the pilot. Beth turned to him.

"It had food . . . water . . . bandages," he said. "It was like a gift from God!"

Beth smiled. Whit hadn't given the backpack to Patrick for them to use. It had been for the pilot.

I'll have to tell Patrick, she thought.

Mrs. Vos gave a glass of water to the pilot.

"Thank you," he said. His hands shook as he took a drink.

Just then, Beth heard voices outside. She sprang up and ran into the hall.

Bernard and Patrick came into the kitchen. They both looked tired.

"I'm so glad you're all right!" Beth cried. Then she froze.

Another man entered from outside. He was wearing a German soldier's uniform.

And he was holding a sleeping baby.

"Dr. Nowak, this is my cousin," Patrick said to the soldier.

Dr. Nowak handed Beth the baby. "She'll sleep for a long time," he said. "I gave her a mild drug to keep her quiet."

"What's her name?" Beth asked.

"We don't know," Dr. Nowak said. "You see,

I brought her here because . . ."

Bernard cleared his throat. "Dr. Nowak? The pilot is waiting." They both hurried out of the room.

"Who's the doctor?" Beth asked Patrick. "Is the German uniform a disguise?"

Patrick said, "No. He's Polish. His country was taken over by the Nazis. They forced him to be a doctor for their troops."

"Oh," Beth said.

"He's a Christian, too," Patrick said. "He wants to help us."

Mrs. Vos hurried into the room. "There she is!" she said, looking at the baby. "We've hidden many Jewish children here. But never one so young!"

"Dr. Nowak said a German soldier saved her life," Patrick said. "He was supposed to make sure no one got out alive. But the soldier couldn't stand to kill a baby. The soldier smuggled the baby out and gave her to Dr. Nowak."

"What about her parents?" Beth asked.

"The father wasn't there," Patrick said. "But we may know where the mother is."

"Dr. Nowak found this address," Mrs. Vos

said. She held up a piece of paper. "It was in the baby's blanket."

Beth peeked over Mrs. Vos's shoulder. The paper had the longest word she had ever seen.

"Nineteen Barteljorisstraat," Mrs. Vos said. "It's a safe house for Jews. It's in Haarlem. About a day's ride from here."

"Then someone should take the baby to her mother," Beth said.

Mrs. Vos looked at the sleeping child. "And soon. The mother may have to leave Haarlem quickly."

"Without her baby?" Beth asked.

"Jews in hiding must often move from place to place. Or they risk being caught," Mrs. Vos said.

"That's terrible," Beth said.

Mrs. Vos nodded. "Come with me," she

said. Beth and Patrick followed her out of
the room.

Mrs. Vos picked up a basket and said,
"You'll need diapers . . . and a bottle . . . and
a blanket."

"What do you mean *we'll* need those
things?" Beth asked. She turned to Patrick.

"We're the only ones who can go," Patrick
said.

"Mr. Vos has to stay on the farm," Mrs. Vos
said. "And I must take care of the pilot."

"Can Bernard come with us?" Beth asked.

"I'm sure he wants to," Mrs. Vos said. "But
you've seen how he looks in a dress. If people
look closely, they'll see that he's a young
man. He could be taken to the work camps."

Beth bit her lip. Then she looked at the
baby. "Okay," she said. "We'll do it alone."

A Warning

Bernard and Dr. Nowak came back to the kitchen.

"The pilot is sleeping now," Dr. Nowak said. "I'll come back in a few days to check on him. Take good care of that baby."

The doctor went out the door and waved good-bye.

Beth said, "He's really brave to help you. He's a hero."

"And so are kids like Mara," Bernard said.

"You and your family are heroes too," Patrick said.

"We're not heroes," Mrs. Vos said. "We're only doing what God wants us to do."

Bernard looked thoughtful. He said, "Some have given up a lot more than we have."

Patrick stared at the dark night beyond the kitchen window. He was worried about the trip.

"Do you think we can do it?" Beth asked quietly.

"I guess we'll find out tomorrow," Patrick said. He tried to keep his voice light.

Mr. Vos appeared in the doorway. "Time to run the radio," he said.

"I hope it's good news this time," Bernard said.

"I fear it's not," Mr. Vos said.

Mr. Vos turned and walked down the hall. Bernard followed. Patrick looked to Mrs. Vos.

"Go with them if you want," she said. "I'll finish packing your things. And I'll watch the baby."

The cousins followed Mr. Vos and Bernard down the hall to a door. They went outside and walked to the back of the house.

Beth pointed toward the woods. Dim light came through cracks in a shed.

Mr. Vos and Bernard went in first. Then Patrick and Beth.

Bernard went to a bicycle that was propped on a stand. A radio was connected to the bicycle. Wire ran from the front wheel to the back of the radio.

Bernard sat on the bike seat and started

to pedal quickly.

A man Patrick had never seen stood near the radio.

Mr. Vos nodded to the man.

The stranger turned to Patrick and Beth. "Who are they?" he asked.

"Friends," Mr. Vos said. "Mr. Smit, would you stand watch while we listen?"

The man nodded and left the shed.

"He lives on a farm nearby," Mr. Vos told Patrick and Beth. "He's another Resistance worker. We share the radio."

As Bernard pedaled, the front wheel spun. But the bicycle stayed in place. They heard the high whine and then a German voice.

Patrick leaned toward Beth. "The radio is powered by the bike," he said.

Beth smiled. "Cool," she said.

The radio was large with three knobs and a dial lit by a dim yellow light. The German announcer's voice was forceful.

Mr. Vos translated. "The police force has been tripled in and around Warmond."

"Tripled!" Bernard said.

Mr. Vos went on, "Dutch citizens are not allowed outside after dark. Anyone who does not follow these rules will be . . ." His voice trailed off.

"What?" Bernard asked.

Mr. Vos said, "They will be arrested and sentenced to death."

The Choice

No one in the shed said a word for a few
moments.

Then Mr. Vos said, "Back to the
farmhouse. But first I need to hide the
radio." He disconnected the wires. Next he
put the radio under the shed's floorboards.

Patrick, Beth, Mr. Vos, and Bernard
quietly walked back to the farmhouse. In
the kitchen, Mr. Vos told Mrs. Vos what they
had heard.

"*Three times* the number of soldiers!" she said.

"I know, Dear," Mr. Vos said.

"The children can't take the baby now," Mrs. Vos said.

"But we have to," Patrick said.

"What about getting to the mother before she leaves?" Beth asked.

Mrs. Vos shook her head. "That was before I heard this news. It's too dangerous."

"They are not safe here either," Mr. Vos said. "The airman is in our home. We could all be arrested or killed if the police find him here."

"I'll go with them to protect them," Bernard said.

"In a dress?" Mr. Vos asked. "No. I won't risk your being sent to the work camps."

Beth groaned. Part of her was afraid to go on the mission. She feared being caught by the Germans. Another part of her thought of the baby and her mother. "We can do it," she said. "We have to get the baby back to her mother."

Mrs. Vos put her hand on Beth's shoulder. "I'm trying to protect you."

"We'll go during the day," Patrick said. "That way we'll look like two normal kids. Then they won't stop us."

"We'll make sure we're there before dark," Beth said. "And if we get stopped, we have our papers."

"But two children carrying a baby is harder to explain," Mrs. Vos said.

"We can hide her in a basket," Beth said.

"And if she cries?" Mrs. Vos asked.

"Then . . ." Beth said and stopped. She didn't have a good answer.

"I have a little more of the medicine from the doctor," Mr. Vos said. "We may be able to keep her asleep awhile longer."

"And if it doesn't work?" Mrs. Vos asked.

Mr. Vos smiled gently. He said, "Perhaps this is when we must have faith in God's protection."

Mrs. Vos sighed. Then she nodded. "All right," she said.

Mr. Vos looked at the cousins. "You leave at first light."

● ● ●

Beth had trouble sleeping that night. Patrick had tossed and turned in the bunk above hers. So she knew Patrick hadn't slept much either.

The gray morning light crept in the window. They both got up at the same time. The entire houseful of people gathered outside to say good-bye.

Everyone except one member of the family.

"Where's Bernard?" Beth whispered to Patrick.

Patrick shrugged. "Maybe he's upset that he can't go with us."

Mr. Vos wheeled two bicycles toward them. "Here you are," he said, smiling. "You get to ride bikes *with* tires."

"Don't most bicycles have tires?" Beth asked.

"Not anymore," Mr. Vos said. "The Germans took all of our rubber. We hid these tires. These bikes are only for emergencies."

Beth bit her lip. This was an emergency.

"Now, listen carefully," Mr. Vos said as he handed them a small piece of paper. A rough map was drawn in pencil. "You'll follow the canals northwest. Look for Haarlem road signs."

Beth and Patrick both nodded.

Mr. Vos had everyone form a circle around them. They all bowed their heads in prayer.

Mr. Vos prayed. He said, "God, we ask that You guide the steps of Beth and Patrick. Give them wisdom. Blind the eyes of our enemies so that our friends will have safe passage. Amen."

Mrs. Vos had wrapped up the baby snugly in a blanket. She placed the baby in the wooden basket on the front of Beth's bicycle.

Then she gave the cousins the backpack.

She told the cousins, "There is food for you. You'll also find a bottle of milk tucked inside. In case the baby wakes up."

"Thank you," Beth said.

"We didn't have diapers, but I put in some parachute cloth to use," Mrs. Vos said. "I think you'll see that God has indeed provided for you."

There was nothing left to do but go. Beth headed down the road with Patrick just behind her.

● ● ●

The streets were empty. Beth didn't see anyone moving. *Maybe they heard the radio warning, too,* she thought. They must be hiding from the Germans.

After a few hours, Beth's legs felt heavy. She wasn't used to riding such a large bike.

She wanted to ride faster, but she couldn't. *What if we don't get to Haarlem in time?* she wondered.

Beth looked at Patrick. He kept glancing back at the street behind them.

"What's the matter?" Beth asked finally.

"There's a motorcycle," Patrick said, "and it's coming up behind us."

The Dutch Police

"Just keep riding," Patrick said. "Act like nothing is wrong."

The motorcycle behind them got louder. Then it sped ahead and cut in front of them.

Patrick and Beth stopped their bicycles.

There were two men in black uniforms riding the motorcycle. One was in the sidecar. He got out and walked toward the cousins.

The man who stayed by the motorcycle said, "You take care of them, Hans. It's a waste of time to question them. They're only children."

Patrick eyed the symbol on their black caps. These weren't German soldiers. They were Dutch policemen.

"We were told to watch everyone leaving the area," Hans said. He stood next to the cousins. "Even children."

Patrick gulped. He tried not to look at Beth's basket.

"Your identification papers, please," Hans said.

Beth and Patrick handed him their cards.

He nodded stiffly. "These seem to be in

order," he said.

He pointed to Patrick's backpack. "What is in that?" Hans asked.

"A few groceries," Patrick said as he handed the backpack to Hans.

"Where are you two going?" Hans asked. He dug into the backpack.

Patrick said, "We're running an errand. For a friend."

"Where does your friend live?" Hans asked.

"Haarlem," Beth said. She pulled the address out of her dress pocket.

Hans looked at the address. His eyes widened.

He knows, Patrick thought. He started

to panic. *He knows Jews go there to hide.*

Then Hans returned the paper to Beth without saying a word. He pulled out pieces of material from the flour sack.

It was silk from the parachute.

Hans gave them a hard stare. "This is silk. Parachutes are made of silk."

"We found it in the woods," Beth said quickly.

"Well? What's taking so long?" the other policeman called from the motorcycle.

From the corner of his eye, Patrick saw movement in the bicycle basket. The baby was stirring.

Beth saw it, too, and she stared at Patrick. She looked panicked. She moved in front of the basket so Hans couldn't see it.

For a second, no one said anything.
Patrick could hardly breathe.

"These children need directions," Hans
said to the other officer. He looked at the
children. "I'll be back."

Beth gently touched the bundle in the
basket.

Patrick stepped up to her.

"Pray the baby doesn't cry," Beth said.

"I am, I am!" Patrick whispered. He
watched the two policemen.

Hans returned with a map. He came
close and pointed down a road. "Now,
this street leads out of town," he said
loudly. It was as if he wanted the other
officer to hear.

Hans glanced over his shoulder. The
man on the motorcycle was looking the

other way.

Hans lowered his voice. He showed
the map to them. "Listen carefully," he
said. "The police station is near the street
you're looking for," he said. "You'll have
to be very careful."

He's trying to help us! Patrick thought.

"I know many Dutch police officers
in Haarlem," Hans said. "If you're in
trouble, tell them you are friends of Hans
Kristoffson."

Patrick nodded.

Hans folded up the map. The baby
made a small whining sound. Hans
looked at the basket, then back at Beth.
"Go. Quickly. And we'll hope your bravery
doesn't get you in trouble."

Patrick opened his mouth to thank

him. But Hans turned and walked away.

Patrick put on the backpack again. He and Beth climbed on their bikes and pedaled away as fast as they could.

They turned a corner and went down a side street. After a few minutes, Beth called out. "Wait!"

Patrick stopped his bicycle. Beth stopped beside him. "I want to check on Miriam," she said.

"Miriam?" Patrick asked.

"That's what I named the baby," Beth said. "Like in the Bible story. Miriam hid her baby brother Moses in a basket."

"Why not call her Moses then?" Patrick asked.

Beth rolled her eyes. "That's not a girl's name," she said.

She unwrapped the bundle in her
basket. Miriam squinted in the sunlight.
She started to cry.

"She needs her diaper changed,"
Patrick said.

"Oh, right," Beth
said. "Those Red
Cross lessons
will come in handy
after all." She got out the parachute
cloth. "I'm glad we have something we
can use for diapers."

"Do you think Hans Kristoffson works
for the Resistance?" Patrick asked.

"Maybe," Beth said. "Mrs. Vos said they
had a friend in the police force."

Beth finished changing Miriam. Then
she fed her with the bottle of milk.

"Here," Beth said, handing the empty bottle to Patrick. She wrapped Miriam up again. "How much farther until we get to Haarlem?"

"It's a long way," Patrick said.

They started riding again. Patrick's mind raced through all the things that could still go wrong.

I hope Mr. Vos's prayer works, Patrick thought.

Haarlem

The sun was just starting to set when the cousins reached Haarlem.

The buildings stood right next to each other. The canals had walkways all around them. The city looked almost cheerful.

It had been a long day. But Patrick was grateful they hadn't been stopped again. So far.

"Watch for German soldiers," Beth said.

"You watch for soldiers. I'm trying to figure out these street signs," Patrick said. The long bike ride had made him tired and cranky.

Just then Patrick saw two men in gray uniforms. They were talking to each other, facing away. But Patrick knew they were German soldiers. If they turned around, they might ask questions.

That's when Patrick heard a high-pitched buzz, like bees. Except this buzz was mechanical.

He looked up. Three gray-and-yellow planes flew overhead. The tail of each plane had a swastika symbol on it.

Nazi planes, Patrick knew. He gulped. *I hope they're not on a bombing raid.*

"Into that alley!" he said to Beth.

They ducked their bikes between two buildings.

Patrick peered out of the alley. The people in the street were all looking up at the planes too.

Patrick wondered, *Those planes won't drop bombs on their own men, will they?*

"Let's wait here until the soldiers are gone," Patrick said.

Beth shook her head. "If we wait too long, we will be out after curfew," she said. "We have to go now."

Patrick checked the street. There were even more men in gray uniforms. He didn't know what to do.

Beth peeked around the corner. "There are people on the street now. We'll blend right in," she said.

She was trying to sound brave. But Patrick could tell she was scared.

Beth peeked into the bicycle basket. Miriam began to whimper.

"I think she's hungry," Beth said. She took the baby out of the basket and rocked her. Miriam's whimper stopped. "Let's hurry."

Beth placed the baby back into the basket. The cousins pushed their bikes into the street. People were still talking about the planes. They glanced up at the sky with worried looks on their faces.

Patrick raced past a group of German soldiers.

"Slow *down*," Beth called to him after the soldiers were behind her. "You don't want me to crash, do you?"

He slowed down to let her catch up. "Sorry," he said.

They turned a corner. Patrick was thankful no soldiers were on this street. He brought his bike to a halt. He got off and walked over to a kind-looking older woman.

"Excuse me," he said. "Can you tell me where this street is?"

He showed the woman the paper with the address.

"Oh yes," the woman said. "That's the street near the police station."

She rattled off a string of directions. Patrick struggled to follow what she was saying.

"Thanks!" Patrick said.

"Now, you children hurry," the woman

called after them. "No one should be out after dark. It's not safe."

Patrick almost laughed. "We know," he called back to her.

● ● ●

Patrick and Beth rode quickly through the streets of Haarlem. As the sun set, darkness spread. The shops began to close. People left the streets.

"Look," Beth said finally. She pointed up at the street sign. It read, "Barteljorisstraat."

"Wait here," Patrick said.

He got off his bike and leaned it against a wall. "I'll find the house. I'll whistle if it's safe to bring the baby," he said.

"Don't leave me by myself!" Beth said.

She got off of her bike too. "What if you get caught?"

"I have papers," Patrick said. "It's the baby who doesn't. And she might start crying."

He was right. They didn't have much of a choice. "Okay," Beth said finally. She stood in front of a bakery. She took Miriam out of the basket and held her close. *I'm not going to let anything happen to you,* she thought.

"I'll be right back," Patrick said.

Beth watched him walk up the street.

Suddenly a soldier stepped from an alley, grabbed him, and pulled him away.

The Gestapo

"Patrick!" Beth shouted. She started to run after him.

"Halt!" a man shouted. "You, girl! Stop!"

Should I keep running? she wondered. But she imagined someone shooting her. She froze where she was.

A man in a black uniform stepped up to her.

Beth swallowed and tried not to look afraid. The man was smoking a cigarette. He wore a red armband. It had a white circle and a black swastika on it. Beth thought the swastika looked like an evil spider.

The man was a member of the Gestapo, the German secret police.

Beth hugged the baby closer to her.

"Why are you out after curfew?" he asked, scowling.

He spoke with a thick German accent. The *w* sound in "why" came out like a *v* sound. Beth had a hard time understanding him.

"I was trying to get in before it started," she said. "That's why I was hurrying."

"Where is the boy?" the officer asked.

"What boy?" Beth said.

"The one who was just with you," he said.

"I don't know where he went," Beth said truthfully.

She prayed that Patrick was all right. She then prayed that *she* would be all right.

"Give me your papers," the officer said.

Beth reached for her ID card.

Then the soldier noticed her bike. "You have rubber tires," he said, kicking them. "Where did you get them?"

"They were a gift," Beth said quickly.

The Gestapo officer stared at the bundle in her arms. He lifted the blanket.

Miriam was asleep. Beth tried to pull her away.

"Does the baby have papers?" the officer asked.

Beth shook her head. Fear tightened her stomach.

The officer glared at her. "Running in the

streets after curfew. No ID for the baby. Rubber tires . . ."

"Like I said, I was trying to—"

"Stop talking and give me your papers," the officer said. His voice was filled with anger.

Beth took the ID card from around her neck.

The officer glanced at it. Then he took a brass lighter from his pocket. He held the flame to the card.

The cardboard quickly caught fire. Soon, it was just ash on the end of a string.

Beth stared in horror. "What are you doing? I can't travel without that card," she said.

"You have dark hair, dark eyes. Who is to say you are not Jewish?" he said.

"I'm not Jewish!" Beth shouted.

The noise woke Miriam. She started to cry.

"Or perhaps you work for the Resistance," the officer said. "Where else would you get the tires?"

He gripped Beth's arm. "You are coming to the police station with me," he said. "Then you will see what we do with Jews and spies!"

Kabang!

The soldier slapped his hand over Patrick's mouth. Patrick couldn't shout.

The soldier dragged Patrick farther back in the alley. Patrick struggled wildly. He punched out at his captor.

"Stop!" the voice said in a harsh whisper. "You'll give us away."

Still, Patrick struggled.

"Patrick, it's *me*!" the voice said. He let Patrick go.

Patrick spun around to face his friend Bernard.

Bernard was wearing a soldier's uniform instead of a dress or farm clothes.

Patrick relaxed and tried to catch his breath. "Where did you get that uniform?" he asked.

"From home," Bernard said. "It was for the pilot. I sort of . . . borrowed it. I couldn't let you leave without me. I've been following you."

"But why did you grab me?" Patrick asked.

"Because the Gestapo agent was watching you," Bernard said.

He turned Patrick toward the street. A man in a Gestapo uniform was questioning Beth.

Patrick started to run toward the street. But Bernard grabbed him.

"Wait," Bernard said. "I have a plan."

Patrick nodded.

Bernard then led Patrick into an apartment building. The boys climbed a central staircase. At the top, they dashed through a door that led to a balcony. They looked down.

Patrick's mouth dropped open. The Gestapo officer was lighting Beth's papers on fire.

"The backpack," Bernard said. "My mother gave you lunch."

"Yes," Patrick said. "This is a strange time to think about eating."

"Give it to me," Bernard said.

Patrick handed the backpack to Bernard. "There's not much left."

Bernard opened it. He grabbed the empty

milk bottle.

"What are you doing?" Patrick asked.

"Just a little Resistance trick," Bernard said.

Bernard took a handful of small white stones out of his pocket. They looked kind of like chalk. He shoved the rocks into the bottle. "Carbide," he said. "We use it in lamps."

"You're going to attack the Gestapo with a *lamp*?" Patrick said.

"No," Bernard said. He brought out a canteen and poured water inside the bottle.

Then he shook up the mixture. "I'm adding water to the carbide," he said. "That way, it will explode."

"You're making a bomb?" Patrick asked.

"It's not a bomb," Bernard said. "Only a distraction. You've heard one before."

Patrick suddenly remembered. "The loud noise in the woods!" he said. "When we were looking for the pilot."

Bernard nodded. "That noise came from one of these." He plugged up the bottle with the rubber cap.

Patrick and Bernard stepped to the edge of the roof.

The Gestapo officer was pulling Beth along the street. Miriam was crying.

A few bubbles formed inside the bottle.

Patrick asked, "How do you know when it's ready to explode?"

"You guess," Bernard said, grinning.

With that, he heaved the bottle over the edge of the roof.

The bottle exploded in midair.

Kabang!

The Gestapo officer jerked toward the sound. He shielded his face.

Patrick watched as Beth broke loose from the officer's grip. She ran toward the alley.

"Come on," Bernard said. "Let's get off the roof before someone sees us!"

Patrick took one last look down.

It was a mistake. The Gestapo officer looked right at him.

For a second, Patrick froze. Then he ran down the stairs behind Bernard.

"You find Beth," Bernard said. "I'll lead the officers away."

"What if you get caught?" Patrick asked.

But Bernard was already gone.

Patrick was alone.

The Watch Shop

Beth ducked into an alley. *What was that noise?* she wondered. *Was it a gun?* She ran faster, holding Miriam tightly.

Miriam was crying.

"Shh. It's okay!" Beth said to comfort her. But it was not okay. She was running for her life.

She glanced over her shoulder. No one was following. Yet.

She stopped in the darkest part of the

alley. Miriam was heavy. Beth had to rest.

The noises behind her continued. She hoped Patrick could escape from the German soldier in all the chaos.

But she couldn't wait for him. She had to save Miriam.

After a few minutes, the shouting stopped. *I have to go back*, Beth thought. *I have to bring Miriam to the safe house.*

Beth retraced her steps. Then she carefully looked out into the street. No one was there.

Beth read the numbers on the buildings as she went along . . . 27 . . . 25 . . .

She wanted to move quickly. But it was hard to read the numbers in the dark.

She passed more addresses . . . 23 . . . 21 . . . 19! She stopped in front of the building.

It was on a corner. The sign on the front said, "Ten Boom: Watches." She turned the doorknob.

"You there!" a voice shouted. "Halt!"

Beth groaned. One more step, and she would have been safe.

A Dutch policeman came around the corner. He had a circle of white hair around his balding head.

The policeman studied Beth. "Do you have anyone with you?" he asked.

"Just a baby," she said.

"A girl with a baby was just being questioned by the Gestapo," the policeman said.

"I haven't done anything," Beth said.

Just then, the door opened and an older woman gazed out at them. Her gray hair was in a bun. Her collar was turned up around her neck.

"What is happening here?" the woman asked. "Why all the noise?"

"This girl was being questioned by the Gestapo when there was an explosion," the policeman said.

"Did she cause it?" the woman asked.

The policeman frowned. "Well, no . . ."

"Then surely the Haarlem police have better things to do than bother children. Go find your bomb-maker," she said.

Miriam cried louder.

"Can't someone make her be quiet?" the policeman asked.

"Here," the woman said. She took the baby from Beth. The woman rocked Miriam until she stopped crying.

The policeman turned to Beth. "Why are you out after dark?" he asked.

Beth's eye went to the sign for the watch shop. *That's it!* she thought.

"I need this watch fixed," she suddenly said. She took the watch from her wrist and held it up. "I thought I could get here before the curfew. But I didn't watch the time."

The policeman frowned. "A joke?" he asked. "You're telling me jokes when I'm about to take you to the station?"

"Don't be silly," the woman said to the policeman. "The watch is broken. It must be repaired. Come inside."

Beth stepped through the door.

The front room was full of watches and clocks of all shapes and sizes. All were set to the exact same time. The ticking sounded like a forest full of crickets.

The policeman followed them. "This is very suspicious," he said.

"Our work doesn't stop because the Germans decide to make war," the woman said. But she was looking at Baby Miriam, not Beth's watch.

The door burst open. Patrick dashed inside. "Beth, I . . ." He froze when he saw the policeman.

Beth thought her heart might stop.

The policeman frowned. "Ah! Another one out after curfew. Are you the boy who caused the explosion?" he asked.

"No," Patrick said honestly. "I didn't."

"I'm afraid I'll still have to take you in for questioning," the policeman said. "Come with me."

The woman stepped forward. "Before you go, I have some pastries in the kitchen. Sugar is a rare treat these days. If you—"

"Sugar . . . ?" he asked. He shook his head. "Don't distract me," the policeman said. He grabbed Patrick's arm.

Then Patrick said, "I'm glad we're going. It will give me a chance to say hello to my friend Hans Kristoffson."

The policeman stopped. "You know Hans?"

Patrick nodded.

"We saw him this afternoon," Beth said.

"Well," the policeman said. He looked toward the door. Then he looked back at the children.

Slowly, he let go of their arms. "Very well, then," he said. "Any friend of Hans is a friend of mine."

He turned to leave. Then he stopped and smiled at the woman. "But a pastry would be nice," he said.

The woman handed the baby to Beth. She disappeared through a door. A moment later she returned with a cloth wrapped around the pastries.

The policeman nodded. "Good," he said. "But be warned. The Gestapo agents are watching everyone. They do not take kindly to strangers. Or those who break curfew."

He lifted a corner of the cloth and broke off a piece of pastry. He popped it into his mouth and hummed.

"You like them?" the woman asked.

The policeman nodded. Then he looked at the children and said, "Conduct your business, and be on your way. Quickly!"

The Hiding Place

The police officer tipped his hat to the woman. Then he walked out the door.

Patrick began to pace. "We have to get out of here."

"No, you don't," the woman said.

"We don't?" Beth asked.

"We have a place here where you can hide," the woman said.

The woman led the cousins to the back of the house. She began to climb a crooked, spiral staircase.

"My name is Corrie, by the way," she said.

"Hello, I'm Patrick," Patrick said.

"Nice to meet you," Beth said. "I'm Beth."

They climbed up to the top floor. Corrie opened the door to a bedroom.

Patrick frowned. It looked like a regular room. *What are we going to do?* he wondered. *Hide under the bed?*

Corrie went to a bookcase along the back wall. She stooped down and slid back a panel.

"Wow," Patrick said. "You can hardly see it!"

"Go inside," Corrie said to the cousins.

The room was dark except for the light

coming in from the doorway.

Patrick's eyes adjusted to the darkness. He saw five people sitting on a cot. There was barely any room for anything else.

The people stared at him. There were three older men and two women. One woman was young and wore a dark dress.

No one spoke. *They all look so scared,* Patrick thought.

Corrie poked her head in behind the cousins and said, "Dora, I believe this bundle is yours." She passed the baby to the woman in the dark dress.

Dora's mouth opened wide. She lifted the blanket an inch. Then she kissed the baby on her cheek over and over and stroked her hair.

Patrick smiled. He looked at Beth. She

was smiling too. *Mission accomplished,* he thought.

Patrick heard banging downstairs.

"They're here looking for the children," Corrie said. "Stay here and *be silent.*" She slid the panel shut. The room was now almost completely dark. Only a little moonlight came through a vent in the wall.

Patrick had never felt so nervous. The others stayed perfectly still where they sat.

The voices from downstairs became louder. Then Patrick heard footsteps up the creaky wooden staircase.

Stopping. Then moving on. Then stopping.

Soon, Patrick heard two sets of footsteps

in the bedroom just outside the hiding place.

The baby stirred. Everyone in the secret room turned to look at Miriam. Dora rocked her gently.

Patrick felt his stomach twist in knots. *We brought Miriam here,* he thought. *Is she going to give us away now?*

Patrick heard the men talking. But the words were too soft to hear clearly. He held his breath.

Then came the tapping.

The Germans seemed to tap on every surface. Distant and then closer. And then they tapped the brick wall of the secret room.

Miriam cooed.

The tapping stopped.

The Jews looked at one another nervously.

Dora placed the tip of her pinkie inside Miriam's mouth. The baby sucked on it quietly.

Moments passed.

No one breathed.

Patrick heard low voices. Then he heard footsteps moving away. A door banged shut.

Patrick sighed. He heard some of the others do the same. Still, no one talked.

Patrick sat down against the wall. He closed his eyes. He felt so tired. But he knew he shouldn't fall asleep.

The next thing he knew, he was being nudged. He opened his eyes. Beth smiled at him.

Corrie had poked her head back into the secret room. "It's safe," she said.

Dora held Miriam close and began to cry. She looked directly at Patrick and Beth. "Thank you," she said. She looked as if she wanted to say more. But her tears kept her from speaking.

● ● ●

Corrie said, "We must feed everyone a nice dinner."

That sounded good to Beth. She was very hungry.

They sat in the dining room with Corrie, her father Casper, and the Jewish guests.

Beth found herself glancing toward the door.

"Don't worry," Corrie said. "We know

what to do if the police come back."

Corrie said that the door was locked. No one could see the dining room from the front window. They also had an alarm system built into the house.

"I don't know how you live like this," Beth said.

"We have many tense moments," Corrie said.

"Then why do you do it?" Beth asked. "You're risking your lives to save strangers."

Corrie's father, Casper, said, "You will remember that Jesus Himself said that, as we help others, we are helping Him. So, in this household, God's people are always welcome."

Beth sipped a spoonful of soup. Then

she said, "But aren't you afraid of getting caught?"

Corrie's father reached for an old Bible. It had a brass cover. He opened the book and turned the well-worn pages.

Beth could see that markings had been scribbled all over the pages.

Corrie's father read a verse aloud. "You are my hiding place and my shield; I hope in Your word."

Corrie nodded. "God doesn't always protect us from danger," she said. "But He's always with us when we face danger. And that's enough."

Patrick lifted his head as if he was listening to something.

Oh no, Beth thought. *What if that noise is from the police?*

Then she heard it, too. A low hum.

The Imagination Station was nearby.
Beth and Patrick went to the window.

"Is something wrong?" Corrie asked.

There was a small patch of yard behind
the house. The Imagination Station stood
there.

Beth looked at Patrick and said, "It's
time for us to go."

● ● ●

Corrie and Casper seemed worried about
the cousins.

"Don't worry," Beth said. "We're safe."

At the back door, Casper extended his
hand. Patrick shook it.

"What about my watch?" Beth asked.

Casper smiled. "It's an honor to fix it
for you. No charge. It will be ready when

you come back," he said.

Beth smiled at Patrick. Patrick knew they would never come back. But there was no way to explain that right now.

Patrick and Beth stepped through the back door and turned one final time to wave to Corrie and Casper.

Patrick wondered about the Vos family, the pilot, and Bernard. He hoped Bernard never had to wear the dress again. He didn't look very good in it.

They climbed into the Imagination Station.

Beth pushed the red button.

Whit's End

"I remember that name," Beth said. She sipped a milkshake back at Whit's End. "Corrie ten Boom."

"She was a very famous speaker and author," Whit said. "She wrote a book called *The Hiding Place*. It was about her family hiding Jews during World War Two. They saved hundreds of people's lives."

"What happened to her?" Patrick asked.

"In 1944, she and some of her family

members were arrested," Whit said. "Her father died days afterward. Corrie and her sister were sent to a concentration camp."

"Oh no!" Beth said.

"Only Corrie lived through the war," Whit said. "Corrie's sister, Betsie, died at the camp."

"That's awful!" Patrick said.

Whit nodded. "Millions of Jews died in that war," he said. "It was a bad time. But it was also a time when good people became heroes. Many ordinary people risked their lives to follow Jesus' command to love others."

"Yeah," Beth said. "It felt good to be able to help people. But it was scary."

"We may not be risking our lives for our

faith right now," Whit said, "but God has useful things for all of us to do."

Beth and Patrick left the shop. Patrick said, "We can't babysit. But maybe we can do something else."

"There's a rummage sale at the church today," Beth said. "It's to help missionaries who live in Africa."

"I'll ask my parents if I can go," Patrick said. "What time is it?"

Beth looked at her digital watch. "Hmm. It's not working," she said.

Patrick reached for the watch. He looked at the blank screen. "I'll fix it."

"Really?" Beth asked.

Patrick said, "No charge."

The cousins laughed together and walked toward home.

Questions about Escape to the Hiding Place

Q: Did the Dutch people support the Nazis?

A: *Most Dutch citizens did not. In 1944, the Nazis cut off the food supply because the Dutch people wouldn't help them. Twenty-two thousand Dutch people died of hunger.*

Q: How did Corrie's house get the special room for hiding Jews?

A: *A man from the Resistance built it for the Ten Booms. He even made the covering of the new brick wall look old and stained so it would be hidden.*

For more info on Corrie ten Boom and World War Two, visit ***TheImaginationStation.com***.

Secret Word Puzzle

Morse code is a series of dots and dashes
that stand for letters. During World War Two,
Resistance workers used Morse code to send
messages over the radio. Crack the code to
find a message.

A •−	G −−•	M −−	S •••	Y −•−−
B −•••	H ••••	N −•	T −	Z −−••
C −•−•	I ••	O −−−	U ••−	
D −••	J •−−−	P •−−•	V •••−	
E •	K −•−	Q −−•−	W •−−	
F ••−•	L •−••	R •−•	X −••−	

1 ·−−· ·−·· ·− −· ·

⬜ ___ ___ ___ ___

2 ··· ···· −−− −

⬜ ___ ___ ___

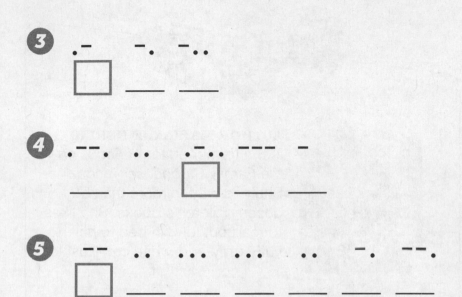

Now take the letters in the boxes and write them here. They spell the reference to the Bible verse that Casper ten Boom read to Patrick and Beth. The word in the boxes is the secret word!

1   2   3   4   5   **119:114**

Go to **TheImaginationStation.com**
Find the cover of this book.
Click on "Secret Word."
Type in the correct answer,
and you'll receive a prize.

119

FOCUS ON THE FAMILY® PRESENTS
THE IMAGINATION STATION

AUTHOR MARIANNE HERING
is the former editor of *Focus on the Family Clubhouse®* magazine. She has written more than a dozen children's books. She likes to read out loud in bed to her fluffy gray-and-white cat, Koshka.

ILLUSTRATOR DAVID HOHN
draws and paints books, posters, and projects of all kinds. He works from his studio in Portland, Oregon.

AUTHOR MARSHAL YOUNGER
has written over 100 Adventures in Odyssey® radio dramas and the children's book series Kidsboro. He lives in Tennessee with his wife and four children. He has been a Cleveland Indians fan for 34 long years.

FOCUS ON THE FAMILY®

No matter who you are, what you're going through, or what challenges
your family may be facing, we're here to help. With practical resources
—like our toll-free Family Help Line, counseling, and Web sites—
we're committed to providing trustworthy, biblical
guidance, and support.

Focus on the Family Clubhouse Jr.

Creative stories, fascinating articles,
puzzles, craft ideas, and more are packed
into each issue of *Focus on the Family
Clubhouse Jr.®* magazine. You'll love the
way this bright and colorful magazine
reinforces biblical values and helps
boys and girls (ages 3–7) explore
their world. **Subscribe now at
Clubhousejr.com.**

Focus on the Family Clubhouse

Through an appealing combination of
encouraging content and entertaining
activities, *Focus on the Family
Clubhouse®* magazine (ages 8–12) will
help your children—or kids you care
about—develop a strong Christian
foundation. **Subscribe now at
Clubhousemagazine.com.**

**Go to FocusOnTheFamily.com
or call us at 800-A-FAMILY (232-6459)**

Start an adventure!
with Focus on the Family

Whether you're looking for new ways to teach young children about God's Word, entertain active imaginations with exciting adventures or help teenagers understand and defend their faith, we can help. For trusted resources to help your kids thrive, visit our online Family Store at:

FocusOnTheFamily.com/resources